Rape A SILENT CRY

Rape A SILENT CRY

By

Tonya Jackson

ISBN: 1-4107-7149-0 (e-book)
ISBN: 1-4107-7150-4 (Paperback)
ISBN: 1-4107-7151-2 (Dust Jacket)

This book is printed on acid free paper.

1stBooks - rev. 07/24/03

Special Mention

Thank You to Elder Gwendolyn Green for allowing the Holy Spirit to lead you to minister unto me, many years ago, that Jesus was going to one day use me to write a book and that it would reach many people.

To Bishop Larry Green Sr. thank you for all your encouragements, corrections, and cheering me on that I may accomplish that what Jesus has for me to do.

To Mommy:

Thanku for giving me life that I may give life to others by the leading of the Holy Spirit and for all that you have done for me!! You did good Mom, You did _Good._

Love Ya!

Toni

Dedication Page

To all of the women and young ladies who thought there was no one to talk to or nowhere to go.

Trust in the Almighty God in the name of

Jesus!

Keep your head up!

<u>Introduction</u>

The story your about to read is at points explicit yet written in the best way of modesty. It does go into the acts that happen during rape and its surroundings.

So, with all respect if you don't feel as though you can handle these situations of rape you now know you may not want to go on any further.

For those that do go on to read, I was inspired by the Lord Jesus Christ to write this book and wanted to share some points that others may not have to go thru this.

God Bless You
&
Thank You
Toni Jackson

Any similar story lines are by total coincidence and are written by the leading of the Holy Spirit. All sentences are based on everyday life.

Contents

Date Rape

In the lives of many young ladies and older women there is a reluctance to trust people they know or meet, who have hurt them, especially males.

These females may have had an absence of a good male role model to teach them right from wrong. Therefore, in situations of date rape that occurs during a friendship, marriage, or long term relationship attribute to their attempt to regain trust in men; unlike the female that had a good male role model.

Moreover, there are occasions were sexual abuse from men becomes apart of some of their lives and trust for some of them may become inevitably destroyed. In addition, denial could set her on a path of constantly trying to trust men; thinking that not all males could possibly be on the same sadistical path.

Based on the points mentioned above I will go further into detail with some explicitness about the acts that may arise during dating or marriage.

I will use throughout each topic, several story lines. The lives of three young ladies who found themselves in positions with men in their lives that within a matter of minutes or time changed their whole outlook in trusting men, on dates or even just knowing them for any length of time within a marriage.

This is where the Silent Cry becomes a part of their lives.

Insomuchas, if you become apart of a sexual assault and you know the male involved, and have accusations of rape brought against him, there is a very high chance that the law will not convict him.

Though there is a 80percent (or higher) rate of rape against women per year there are many that still have not spoken up out of fear and the possible disbelief from family members and the court room, (judge, jury) if brought to trial. This is because most juries would believe since there was an association by short/long term relationship, that rape is not likely. Somehow, believing the answer was really yes and not no.

These young ladies in which will become a great part of the whole truth of Rape: A Silent Cry names are Kelly a 14 year old girl, Jayna a 27 year old lady and Susan a 24 year old married woman.

Kelly is a female who was striving to achieve that perfect love she had heard about many times from her girlfriends. All alone as a teenager with really no one she felt she could talk to she began reaching out for love from male companions. This seemed that it would be the best remedy for the void she had in her life, the lack of love from a father figure. Little did she know that for the cost of love, from a male, would cost her virginity.

Losing her virginity, as a teenager made her feel that there was no danger or harm done especially because her girlfriends spoke so highly of their own personal experiences.

Kelly began her first intimate involvement with a guy named Allan; which gradually evolved into the loss of her virginity.

Kelly had intercourse with Allan with just an inkling of an idea of what was going to happen or even how. With the insertion of his manhood broke her skin (hymen), upon the entrance into her precious jewels causing her to bleed. When the whole act of intercourse was over Kelly realized that she was bleeding. Because of the lack of communication with her parents she just assumed that her menstrual cycle had started for that particular month. She thought to herself, "good at least I am not pregnant". Without recognizing that it was a sign of losing the most precious gift, God had given to her.

At such a high price for love (which is priceless) Kelly began finding out that she was only setting herself up for many pitfalls of hurts. Within her innocence and naiveness she found herself in the first of many relationships where her love was the only thing that kept the relationship together. And eventually everything between them just ceased without warning.

Kelly's future relationships were more emotionally painful than she could ever imagine. The next two relationships which were in succession, she found to be ones with a sense of caring about her feelings but in all Kelly found out that she was not the only female involved with the guy she was going out with. This was something she had discussed with each of her companions in previous conversations, whether she was the one and only or not! Of course their response was she was the one and only, with the intent to keep her holding onto something that had no substance or future.

Left alone with now an even more shattered vision of what she was really looking for in a relationship Kelly's heart was broken in what seemed to be in more pieces than when she had been torn in the involvement with Allan.

There was a period in Kelly's life that she felt there was a need to step back and take a look at the downhill emotional roller coaster she was riding. When she did look back at all the wrong moves she had made Kelly felt that she could improve the odds of her success in the love game she had been <u>playing</u>, by just simply being tougher within her personality, playing harder to get, standing firmer in her decision-making with the male factor involved.

Kelly was now content with the decision she made, which by the way was made in a fairly short period, almost as though she was missing out on something. Instead of healing and maturing she stepped forward into another relationship.

With the span of approximately three years she met a young gentleman, Andy, who cared for her more than she had seen in past involvements with guys. The one thing she noticed that did not seem to disappear was the fact that he also wanted to have sex with her.

Kelly expressed how she felt about each time she met someone (of the male gender) the subject on having sex never seemed to cease. After talking about it, they both felt her feelings didn't seem to play a major role in the place of sex. Kelly was now forced with the judgement of either standing by her decision or giving in; after all she was still very young. If she settled for not having sex there was a great possibility of losing him. And in letting her guard down would result in not keeping up her standards she had set and a huge chance that the love that she felt she had found could still end up like all the other times. Kelly's final choice as to whether she would or not have sex came down to simply she would.

With what seemed to be a forceful outcome all went well and love between them appeared to be escalating until one-day Kelly's way of being tough interfered with what Andy wanted.

He wanted to take Kelly back into what appeared to be a blocked off vacant lot, were a house used to stand in order for him to get his rocks off (rubbing against her jewels back and forth with his manhood fully clothed). This is known as grinding or dry sex. She didn't want to because she was afraid that someone would see her going back into this area and would come to find out what they were doing. Because she stood her ground and continued to say no, she didn't want to grind with him, back in an area that seemed to be nothing but trouble, he picked up a large stone with sharp rigid edges threatening her. Saying, "if you don't cooperate I'm going smash you with it." Out of fear of dying and still not wanting, to lose him, she went along with what he told her to do.

During the whole act of Andy trying to reach his peak of ecstasy Kelly just stood there, leaning against the wall, not going along with what he was doing until he said "Kelly what's wrong with you? You better act like you know and move your body to make me feel good!" So she proceeded and started moving along. She had no feeling in the act whatsoever. The feeling of love was not present, she felt used, belittled, alone and empty.

Before leaving the vacant lot he briefly kissed her cheek and began walking out. Kelly stood limp against the wall for a few seconds as if to gather her feelings first and then her thoughts as to what had just happened. Then she followed along when Andy called her to come on. She was in a state of a daze.

Little did Kelly know or understand about these occasions she had been experiencing, but she was allowing herself to be conditioned, a psychological terminology, into the fear of losing male companions. Conditioning is a learned behavior of a particular situation that after it has been practiced continuously over a period of time with the same result it appears to the individual to be a normal reaction.

Kelly's relationship continued with Andy but the occasions of him wanting to be outside grinding on her increased to the point of being, outrageously audacious. He would do it at train stops, on the stairwells and behind houses. Kelly, at these times felt as though she was numb, as though her feelings fell asleep while she was standing awake about the whole grinding act.

As time went on, it seemed apparent that Andy would resort to this manner of behavior when he could not figure out where to go to have sex.

Over the years Kelly and Andy were together there were many times where he would call her to come to see him giving her the impression that they would spend quality time together. But much to her surprise the phone call was a sex call. By the time she met up with him he would take her to a place he set up, by way of male friends, to use their place for a period of time, to have sex.

The first time Andy planned this secret sex call caused Kelly to experience that numb feeling which was becoming all too familiar, as if she were just having a normal reaction.

When they arrived at the apartment that Andy had gotten keys for there was no pretense. He took her straight to the bedroom told her to take off her clothes because he did not have much time. She reluctantly stood there with the thought that she didn't know whose bed this was and she was not going to take off her clothes. When Andy saw that see was not going to cooperate he began to take her clothes off himself. Kelly's reaction was one that may as well have been a manikin's because she didn't move, with the exception of Andy moving her arms and legs to get the clothes off and he walked her across the room to the bed leaving the pile of clothes where she stood. He did his business, got up, got dressed and told her to hurry up and get dressed so they could get out of there.

As you can see Kelly's view of how good intimacy should be was becoming very bleak as well as tarnished accompanied by the damaging of her already low self esteem, feeling that she was not worth anything but sex.

Eventually, Kelly decided just to go on about her life and not be bothered anymore with Andy especially after they got into a fight one night because she just out and out didn't budge toward his advancement to have sex.

By this time she had only been spending time with him sporadically so it didn't have a great affect on her.

Sometime went by and Kelly met someone by the name of Drib. She felt he was handsome. They exchanged phone numbers. Kelly felt that maybe she would just add him to the host of phone numbers she had been collecting over some time, numbers which she used from, time to time just to hold conversation when she was bored. It didn't go that way. They began visiting one another and talking a great deal on the telephone.

Though Kelly's acquitance with Drib was very short lived it also involved having sex. This association consisted of not only sex but a gun was also comprised; a 44 caliber-automatic, with a 14 bullet clip. He pointed it at Kelly one day to intimidate her into having sex with him. That was not the only time he used it, alongside that he would point it at any given time for whatever bazaar reason he felt. There was a time that just because she was talking to an old acquitance there was almost a great big shoot out. From this nightmare of what was so innocent Kelly made her mind up that she did not want to be associated with Drib anymore.

A few days had gone by and she expressed to him that she did not want to be bothered anymore, while standing outside of his house. He said it was okay and they walked away from each other. Kelly's girlfriends were nearby and she continued the night on with them. Until Drib decided to go into a neighboring house, he went into the back bedroom and pointed his gun out of the window to shoot at Kelly and whomever she was with. But by the Grace of God's mercy she recognized the gun being slipped out of the window and she and her girlfriends ran for cover behind a truck parked very close by.

For once, in what had been a long time, Kelly had the time and chance to spend with her girlfriends and wouldn't you know it something like this happens.

The personal effects of this relationship between Kelly and Drib had long-term effects upon Kelly. Many of her nights were riddled with dreams of being shot at, being killed or even being shot multiple times, at most the number of bullets she could remember entering her body in the dreams was fourteen, left laying on the floor of someone's house for dead with no one to help her.

Though these dreams happened more often than not Kelly managed to keep her right state of mind. And for the first time in a long time she had found a friend she could confide in. This was what she believed helped her thru all of those tough spots she had experienced until now.

Her name was Tee. Kelly felt comfortable telling her intermost feelings to Tee. There were often times Kelly would feel that no one cared about her especially the male gender. She would cry all the time and ask herself what was wrong with her that she had so many problems holding on to or just even being able to capture a good male relationship the way she seen so many other girls do while growing up. She began to think she was not pretty enough, smart enough and that she would never attain the type of love she had been looking for so long.

Being able to talk to Tee allowed Kelly to have a broader view as to why things were not going the way she wanted them to. Tee explained, from her point of view, that Kelly should never give her whole heart the way she'd been doing in past relationships. She rationalized that while in a relationship you should keep some of your heart for yourself, for example: "It's okay to give maybe 80 percent of your heart but keep 20 percent for yourself." Kelly began to think and these words seemed to have the remedy of not being hurt so badly after such unions as the ones she had in times past. She would soon find out how well this stagtegy would work.

There was somewhat of a joy within Kelly. She knew he had come this far, with the knowledge of sexually transmitted diseases (STD) and she had never experienced this type of trauma. She felt if she had to go thru something such as STD's she would have really lost her mind. But with the peace mind and absence of STD'S she guarded her heart and was willing to try the game of love once again.

In the months of healing Kelly regrouped her thoughts took the pace, which she thought was slow, and began dating Roger. She decided the best way to go about getting to know him would be to talk on the phone then graduate to visiting. Everything went well with guarding her heart so she would not be hurt again. What Kelly did was not allow herself to show any of her feelings or for that matter not even recognize or pay attention to what she really felt. Kelly encamped her heart with what seemed like the highest brick wall surrounded by enclosed steel barriers. This helped her to deal a totally different way concerning her feelings.

She became completely nonchalant toward negative feed back from men and even women. Her way of being kind tended to become nasty. Almost anyway that appeared justifiable worked for Kelly as long as she did not get hurt.

She felt she was in a good mode now and well protected. She began visiting Roger and even hanging out with him sometime. The first few times of going over to his house were fun, quite, and different. And that was all Kelly wanted a friend that would treat her for who she was and not for how much sex he could get out her. One day Roger bumped into Kelly at the bar so they partied a little bit, had a drink or two, he then took her by the arm suggesting lets get out of here, with a little hesitation Kelly put on her coat she had been wearing before she came inside the bar, it was cold and snowing outside. She went with Roger not really knowing where he was leading her off-to. They came outside started walking down the street that's when she realized they were going to his house. She didn't have any fear of what may happen because he had shown her she could trust him. As usual when they both entered the house they walked straight up to the bedroom this is where Roger felt most comfortable, it was what he called his dominion. He began resting his clothes, that is to say taking them off to get comfortable since he was just coming in from work, he turned on the music then he sat on the bed with Kelly leaning over to kiss her, she received him and kissed him back. It seemed like the longer they kissed the deeper the passion was and the more intense the intimacy became. Roger, unlike any of the other times he had spent with Kelly, began to unbutton her blouse and to take off her bra and Kelly exclaimed, "No I don't want to take off my clothes!" but he didn't listen just like all the other times Kelly cried out _NO_. At that point she became very serious and began to pull away but because he was such a big guy and she was no more than 140 pounds, there was no getting away. Kelly's body fell limp and despondent by the time he had taken off all of her clothes. Roger proceeded to caress her with his lips over her body and then inserted his manhood into her jewels. He was very what she felt like, very wild with her and it seemed as though it went on for more than 2 hours. After the whole ordeal of sex was over, which she made no act to participate; he rolled over and fell fast to sleep, not saying one word to Kelly.

Kelly lay opposite from him with her back turned to him curled in what looked like a fetal position. She could not believe that this had happened again. It was almost like it was normal and was suppose to happen this way.

While she lay there awake and alone she was angry more than anything and she felt used. And what made it even worst lying awake, was the music that had been turned on, that had rhythm and beat, seemed to now fit the mood to what had occurred, it sounded like Avant Guarde, but as it went on it sounded like a nightmare, just like she was in.

The game Kelly played in shielding her heart worked for the most part when she was with Roger. Though he had sex with her without her consent Kelly kinda swept it under the rug, as if her feelings didn't matter, and ignored all her negative feelings toward Roger. She continued to express to Roger that she wanted their relationship to be more than visiting each other and for the finale having sex. He went along with her wishes for weeks at a time. One Friday evening Kelly stopped by to see Roger he was spending a quite evening watching television, he was very surprised to see Kelly when he answered the door. When Kelly came in he received her with a warm welcome. They talked for hours, held one another, even gave each other a few intimate kisses. Before they knew it was about 4:30, 5:00 a.m. Without any hint of what was going to happen next Roger lost control of being a good gentleman and began taking off Kelly pants. Once again she was fighting to keep her clothes on. She lost the battle of keeping her sexuality to herself with his insertion. Roger knew Kelly was not on any type of birth control so within the two minutes the act lasted, at the peak of his pleasure; he did what he called a quick draw to assure that she would not get pregnant.

Kelly rolled over this time and a tear fell from her eye but right at this moment she knew she was pregnant. Little did she know that it was Jesus letting her know what was to come in the near future.

At that time while Kelly was now in what seemed to be a normal position, a fetal position, Roger had gotten up and hurried along, to get ready for work, and to take Kelly home, in order for him to get to work on time.

For about a month and a half Kelly didn't call or see Roger. During that time she went for her check-up at the gynecologist. She had been counting her days since her last period and by this time it was up to 46 days since her last cycle began. The test that had been taken to see if Kelly was pregnant was positive 6 weeks. This was not really a surprise to Kelly especially because she had heard God's voice that morning after the incident with Roger, telling her before hand she was pregnant (she heard his voice not even being saved from her sins).

Kelly knew now she had to tell Roger. They made arrangements to see each other on a Saturday night with him not knowing her agenda. That night came and when Kelly told him he didn't want to receive what she had told him about her pregnancy. He talked to her and expressed how he really felt, of course he was angry and in a state of denial: He explained, "that he would get in touch with her to give his final decision," as to whether he wanted to go along with her pregnancy, which as it turned out, he didn't want to go through it. The night Roger called to give Kelly his answer of no made her feel as though her feet had fell from underneath her. After she hung up the phone she began to cry, she then called Tee telling her to come meet her she needed someone she could talk to. By the time she got half way around the corner Tee had already ran to meet her knowing that something was terribly wrong. She immediately gave her a hug and Kelly really began cry sorely, giving all the details as to what had just happened with Roger. She explained tearfully, "Roger no longer wants to be bothered with me and he actually said, not to call him or if I see him on the street not to speak to him." This hurt more than anything she could imagine. Mostly, because Kelly never wanted any children from the beginning and she felt if she did ever get pregnant she did not want to do it all alone, she found herself right in the middle of what she never wanted to happen. After that night Roger saw her about 1 to 2 times more within 3 years. To make things even worst Kelly found out she was carrying triples, two girls and a boy. This broke Kelly emotionally, she was depressed, confused and all alone and not knowing what she should do, so she prayed about it, asking Jesus to show her what to do with the babies. Whether she should get rid of them, by way of abortion or adoption, the answer came out to be, keep them.

The constant looking for love never ceased. But one thing Kelly began to see and know was that she was raised in a Christian atmosphere and in growing up she stayed in church and it was now time to start heading back that way. Because that would be the only _real_ love she would ever know in her life.

Although she knew this she met someone else and this experience was unlike all the rest, without usury. His name was Ken and he loved her and treated her with respect but in the end he could not accept that he was falling in love and left without warning.

Kelly always believed that God wanted her to see that not everyone was out use her and that was why Ken came into her life.

After that point Kelly got saved, becoming a born again Christian and realized that the love she had been looking for all along was standing right there waiting to be accepted into her heart and His name is *JESUS.*

As stated earlier in this book not all women are single, that experience the trauma of rape. This is true in the case of Susan a 27-year old married woman.

She got married at the age 25 to her husband Victor. The relationship between Susan and Victor could not have been any better than it was in the first two years of their marriage where there was caring, gentleness and kindness this gradually turned into situations of carelessness towards Susan. Victor began to come behind her to snatch her by her hair to kiss her whenever he got the urge to kiss her. The kiss, it was cold without any emotion, and abrupt. Totally unusual from what she had become accustom to.

Susan didn't quite understand why Victor had initiated such behavior, especially because it was nothing he had done before, even during their courtship. She supposed that his work had become stressful and this was his outlet.

Weeks went by and Victor's aggressiveness escalated into snatching her clothes off, anywhere in the house, having sex with her vigorously. Until she was so stiff and in so much pain that he could not reach his peak of ecstasy. Her inner legs became badly bruised. The entrance to her jewels swelled to the point that it had closed up and had to be packed with ice. Tears of shock and hurt poured from Susan's eyes but Victor didn't appear to have any remorse at all for her.

Susan was afraid, depressed and felt hopeless. She knew that she didn't have anyone she felt she could talk to. Particularly, because Victor had threatened her not to tell anyone, because it would be worse the next time.

She figured out that some of this behavior was attributed from the sudden pressures and demands placed upon him in the work place.

Now Susan knew if she did go to talk with her father and or her brothers she would lose her husband, due to death. Susan felt as though her world had crumbled all around her and there was no firm foundation. Either she could stay with Victor and hope his instability would sustain to normal levels of caring or leave which would indicate to her father and brothers something was definitely wrong, then she would have to really hope they didn't hurt him in any way.

While time went by, approximately 1 to 2 weeks, Susan thought earnestly over her situation. During that time Victor came home one night drunk, she knew that he had been out drinking, at this point Susan feared for her life. She didn't know what to do so she hurried along, turned off the lights, got into the bed and pretended as if she were asleep for a long period of time, before Victor made it up the stairs to their master bedroom. He noticed that her head was buried under the covers therefore he went into the master bathroom to remove the stench of alcohol from his body.

Susan lay there in bed, under the many blankets, because winter had not broken yet, and gave a sigh of relief. Her thoughts were, "he's not going to bother me! He's too drunk to do anything straight let alone have sex".

Much to her surprise the shower he had taken invigorated and stimulated him more than she had hoped. And in his mind he was capable of doing anything just as if he had not gotten drunk. He climbed into their king size bed, moved over until he reached Susan on the other side and began to kiss her until it hurt. That wasn't enough he began to bite her neck, not small and loving nibbles but large harsh bites that left teeth marks on her neck. The process continued, instead of unbuttoning her nightgown he ripped it open fondled her bosom with his mouth until they began to tear. Then the inevitable occurred he did things with his mouth he had never done before, he then entered her with his vigorous acts as he had done in the recent past.

Just as anyone that has been conditioned to an activity or behavior Susan was no different in her response toward what was being done to her. She was motionless, had no sentiment, even though this was her husband, she stared out into what seemed like space hoping it would be over very soon.

unlike Kelly, Susan did not cry out to God as her Lord and Savior Jesus Christ, she carried this load all by herself. Susan's **Cry was very silent,** only Victor Susan and Jesus knew about it, to whom she didn't know she could look up to heaven and cast all her cares upon him for he cares for her (I Peter 5:7) KJV.

Christian Walk

On the night before Kelly decided to give her life to Christ it was almost like any other night with the exception of going out with her girlfriend to a nightclub. They danced, mingled a little with the crowd, ate and drank. This was something Kelly felt she owed to herself.

Though the music played loudly it was yet a calm and quite atmosphere. Before she realized, it was closing time for the club, 2a.m. She was a good distance from home but it didn't matter this nite because she had gotten a rent-a-car for the weekend. This enabled her to get home fairly quickly and safely, even though she had two lightweight drinks. Her girlfriend drove also and they went their separate ways.

Once Kelly arrived home she realized that she had made plans with her family members to go to church service the next morning, which was Sunday.

When Kelly got up on Sunday she made further arrangements as to how she would meet up with everyone that was going. The decision was her family would ride together and Kelly would drive the car she had. Kelly felt this was best she could then leave at her own convenience going and coming back. Especially, because they were leaving from a different location, about 20 minutes from where she was. It was settled she would meet everyone at the church.

When Kelly arrived, upon entering the church, the music that was being played was that of a different beat than she had been listening to the night before and for that matter the past years of her life. She found a seat and instead of getting right into the service she kept looking at the door each time someone came in, hoping her family would be there very soon, because this was only her second time there and she didn't know anyone in this large place.

Eventually, she stopped paying attention to the door. Then the minister of the hour made an altar call. With everything in Kelly's natural power she was going to stay right in the seat she had found. Without any thought she got up out of her seat and walked to the front of the church for the altar call, this was for anyone that didn't know Jesus as his or her personal Lord and Savior. While standing there two other people came up too. The minister continued to speak as the Holy Spirit of the Lord lead him to do so. He then walked from the pulpit to talk to Kelly and spoke as the Lord told him to tell her, "don't leave here today without accepting Jesus into your heart because it maybe your last chance." Then the Elders of the church took Kelly and those who chose to change the ways of life for Christ back into a room, in another area of the church. The Elders (these are the leaders of the church that are directly under the Pastor) spoke to them concerning salvation, deliverance from sins, and accepting Jesus into their hearts. It was a matter of letting Jesus know all of their sins they had committed up until this point and that they wanted to give him all of their sins and hurts for the promise of life eternal with Jesus. Kelly thought to herself **WOW!** Is that all? Is it that easy? Here's a man that I can get very intimate with in the spirit and in truth and he won't hurt me, take advantage of me, abuse me, lie or use me as a piece of meat that could be used as a sex object, she felt this was the greatest thing of all, so she went for it.

The Elders of the church then took them back into the sanctuary as new children in Christ. Then the doors of the church were opened, that is to say if they didn't have a church they belong to as members they were welcome to join this branch of Zion.

Kelly began to cry and without understanding to why she was crying. The tears rolled and rolled from her eyes continually and she could not stop them.

She and the other two people all joined as members. At that point the whole congregation was invited to make a line and welcome their new converts/members.

Kelly felt this was wonderful everyone that came around to the front of the sanctuary either shook her hand or gave her a hug, something she didn't have in a very long time from anyone. She cried even harder, the tears didn't seem to want to stop.

At the dismissal of church service Kelly said, "Goodbye" to those she had met while she was there. Her family never showed up.

While she drove away in the rent-a-car, a white 1991 Cougar with 4 doors, she never dreamed it would lead her to take this direction in life. She thought about all that was said and done. In pursuit of driving the car, it felt like a feather going about into the direction she instructed it to go. She also realized that the feelings she had felt much of her teenage years, now in her mid 20's, up until that day were the weights of the world she never dismissed or discharged by reason of not telling anyone all of the things she was going through back then. Now Kelly had given them to Jesus and felt 100 percent better. The tears played in a great deal of her cleansing, from all of her scared emotions.

In the days to come Kelly already knew what was expected from her concerning her new walk of life, having salvation in her heart. Immediately, when she returned home, she knew from when she was a little girl and went to church service that the music she had been listening to would no longer be apart of her life, because it was worldly music, this would be a sacrifice but she did not mind because she wanted to do what pleased Jesus. Some of the types of music: R & B, Rap, Punk Rock, Blues etcetera, anything that did not glorify the name of Jesus. Even if it meant taking away all of her old worldly habits, drinking liquor of any sort, cursing, lying, cheating, deceiving, having sex, before marriage, even though she had it in the past she was willing to wait until that time, of marriage. (Colossians 3:1-17) KJV

Kelly didn't talk to anyone about her good news for about a week then she broke her silence.

She became more humble, kinder, patient, and learned how to treat people better. A few of the many ways of Christ she allowed herself to be conformed to at this point.

One of the more challenging things for Kelly was learning not to have male companions as she had in the past. After about 8 years she felt she was strong enough in her spirit man to have a male she could talk to.

Kelly did meet someone his name was Morton. Their friendship started off with long conversations. One night Morton saw Kelly while he was driving down the street, he stopped, talked with her for a while then they both noticed how late it had gotten. They were talking for about an hour and a half. He then asked her would she mind if he took her home, she felt comfortable with his presence so she said, "yes". Since she was on the porch visiting a classmate from college she had to go into the house to say goodbye, also to collect her belongings.

Kelly was now on her way home and was somewhat happy she didn't have to call a cab.

Upon Kelly arriving home their conversation continued as if she had not reached her destination. Once Morton noticed he was sitting there idol just listening then responding, he pulled out of the parking spot he had drove into, with her permission, proceeding to drive until he came to a very scenic, serene place surrounded by pretty flowers, and a lake with the moon shining on it allowing the night to take its course because it was such a nice summer nite. They both began to realize that they were hungry so Morton said, "come on I know a place that stays open all night." So they went to get something to eat. By this time Kelly felt the time really was getting too late, it was 2:30 a.m. She told him to take her home because this was now really out of her normal limits of being out. He respected her wishes and proceeded in the direction to take her home. This made Kelly happy because he seemed to pay attention to her wishes. On the way to her house he made a statement that he needed to stop home for a minute but he would take her home a soon as he ran into his house and came right out. This was okay to Kelly because he doubled parked and left her in the car with it on. It took all of 5 minutes that was a relief to Kelly.

She finally arrived home. At that point she began to get out of the car and he asked her could he come in. That question made her slow her pace for a few seconds to think about what he was exactly asking. Given their time spent together and his commitment in showing her his respect she said, "Okay", without any second thoughts. They both entered the quite house, which was minus Kelly's triples, whom where now away in their 1st year/semester of college. She offered him a seat in the living room while she got situated in putting her belongings away, she turned on the gospel music before leaving the room just to remind him the kind of girl she was.

Kelly now re-entered the living room continuing their talking. The only difference was he started to kiss her in her mouth. Kelly thought to herself, "This is nasty; I don't know him like that." So she began to verbally express herself, asking him what was wrong with him, did he loose a section of his brain or something, why was he acting like this, especially because he tried to force her mouth open by squeezing her jaws with his fingers. That didn't stop him. Her eyes got very large as if she were in shock and she began to fight Morton to get him to stop, but that just seemed to fuel the moment of his so called passion. His mode escalated to turning off the lamp that sat adjacent to the sofa, applying more force to getting Kelly to move and to cooperate with him moving into the middle of living floor away from any objects she may have been able to clug him with. He went straight into action not stopping for one moment even in the process of pulling her clothes from her body. He held her arms with one hand and used the other hand to take her clothes off, bottom only. He did things razzeling to her then he decided to penetrate as a man would into her jewels. Kelly lay there not wanting to believe this was happening, so she blocked it out of her emotions so she would not feel any hurt. This is what allowed her to stay friendly with Morton. What she didn't realize she allowed some of her old habits back into her heart and her life, the act of conditioning. Which come under the category of mind control. That very next day she allowed him to take her out to brunch, paying no attention to the reality of the whole situation. This permitted their relationship to continue on. She began missing lots of church services.

Kelly began to see things for what they really were after a short period of time, this was not right and she realized she was sinning all over. She had to let Morton know it was over between them and their relationship had to cease. It was at this space in time that she noticed her focus was altered. She also explained to him, even though he was very familiar with how her Christian walk should be, although he was not active in his own Christian walk. (Amos 3:3 KJV: "How can two walk together unless they both be agreed"). This verse made it easy to proceed in her walk alone.

She started attending services, reading her bible and praying the way she should. These things are essential in the Christian walk and she could not set them aside in order to do what she use to do, because, she would find herself in the same predicament. She also had to go thru deliverance from all those evil things she allowed back into her life. Kelly's life was much better once she let go of her heavy load; Letting Jesus carry it, not she. But one thing was still against her, Morton was trying very hard not to let go of the relationship with Kelly.

It was approximately 3 months and Morton stopped by out of the blue, right before she was leaving to go out. It was daytime; the sun was shining brightly through the open blind at the window and in spite of that it didn't stop Morton from trying to take off Kelly's panties from under her jean skirt. This started without any warning just, __BAM!__ Kelly held on to her panties and her skirt with everything in her being. Pushing him, tying her legs together, everything she could think of, while up against the living room wall for support, in her fight for victory. It didn't work. He pinned her down with his hands and his weight to the floor once he got her away from the wall leaving marks on the white wall. Once he got her panties off he began to razzle her.

Morton never even thought for one moment about the window being a witness to his harsh act.

The whole act was over and Kelly was steaming MAD. She got herself together to go out while he sat on the sofa. When she returned to the living room she turned on the music so loud she could not hear Morton talking to her. This allowed all of Kelly's frustration and anger to vent without snapping or hurting him in any way. He got angry and left, which was good for Kelly because she was ready to go anyway.

Later that night after she went shopping she went to prayer service and when she started praying she began to cry not letting anyone around her to see her emotion or even know what was wrong for those who saw the tears. These tears she realized were okay to cry because it was the beginning of another cleansing process.

Kelly was very determined to get on the right track. She continued to take all of the necessary steps that would strengthen her walk in Christ.

After about 9 months the worse that could ever happen to Kelly happened. Morton stopped by as he had in the past months to talk so she answered the door. She had been sleeping, it was the early, early hours of that Sunday morning in June and Kelly thought nothing of it because it was something he had done many times before. Mostly when something was on his mind and he wanted someone to talk to he felt comfortable with. Kelly sat on the sofa in a knot, hoping he would be finished talking very soon, since she had to go to work in a few hours. It was almost like an instant replay from the very first time she allowed him into her place, he raped her again. The only difference this time was she prayed vehemently against him because she realized Jesus was on her side and Kelly on his, unlike before, now she was complete.

The only problem with that was though she prayed she was outside of the will of God: she never should have let him in regardless of the situation. Which means, as long as she was walking and moving in the parameters of the Holy Spirit no evil could touch her, (Psalms 91) KJV: as soon as you get into your own way of seeing and doing things, bad things can happen to you similar to Kelly.

In the following hours, which were about 4 hours, Kelly went to work without any emotion all day long. Directly after work she decided to catch the ending part of Sunday afternoon church service. Within minutes of her entering the door, the minister of the hour began to let the Holy Spirit minister through him, to Kelly. Without him knowing what had happened in the earlier part of the day he called her up to the pulpit speaking directly to her saying "Thus saith the Lord, you are somebody worth waiting for, you are not A PIECE OF MEAT out for the slaughter at will" (this was encouragement that Kelly needed to stay on track.) See, the devil had a trap of destruction that she may not reach her potential in Christ. Kelly cried even as he prophesied to her, still not telling him what had happened. Once she started crying the tears just rolled from her eyes, she allowed them to do so not caring who saw her crying. The only thing was that there were so many tears backed up inside of her it was only a few times, for a few minutes, that she stopped crying after that. Many tried to cheer her up but couldn't, the tears just kept coming down her face. Her Pastor offered to take her home but she didn't even trust him **that day**. On the way home on the bus she prayed the whole way for her tears to stay inside until she got in the door. Low and behold that's how it happened. Once she got in the door at the early hour of about 8:00 p.m. she got ready for bed, got in it, curled up in a fetal position, cried and sobbed until she felt asleep.

The path of total healing had to start for Kelly just as for anyone else who has been through any type of trauma such as RAPE. Kelly wrote Morton a letter that same week he raped her. The situation, this time was more devastating than any of the other times she was raped. That was one of the reasons she decided to write him to tell of her pain and anger. She knew if he knew who the letter was from he may have not read it. So she wrote in such a way that he had to read almost the entire letter before knowing who had written the letter.

From that day forward whenever Kelly's male aquitances stopped by for even just a few minutes, coming inside (married or unmarried) she felt nervous and scared but she didn't allow her emotions to show. Most times she knew if they would be stopping by while in the vicinity of her house. But before they got there that was when she got a nervous stomach and sometimes a headache.

She realized that this was a tough road of healing she had to go through but she was willing to go through it.

Kelly also recognized that she was going to have to learn to love and how to be loved unconditionally, with Jesus' AGAPE love, and this would be the road to recovery. In doing this it was about trusting God. Because if she didn't she knew that it would never work trying to do it all by herself.

In my introduction of the characters/women I mentioned three women I would be writing about, the last one's name is Jayna a 27 year old woman.

Jayna is a woman who really loved the Lord Jesus and was sold out (submissive) to do his will. There was one weakness though, as with some Christians until they are delivered from those things of the flesh, she allowed herself to have a male aquitance that was strictly platonic. You may think to yourself that's okay as long as it stays that way. The fact is when you're totally sold out for Jesus your interest should be in him until he sends the man he (Jesus) has picked out for you. Therefore, Jayna was outside of the will of God.

As with Kelly, Jayna also lacked love in her younger years. As Jayna had done up until the day she got saved, she kept a male friend on the side for various worldly reasons. Her exception now was she was not willing to deal with men the way she did when she was not saved.

The friend that Jayna had now his name is, Mark. Jayna liked being around him most, though he was not saved, besides her girlfriends at times.

Jayna allowed herself to fall in love with Mark. This happened rather easily because Mark was a real gentleman, easy to get along with, conversations never had any type of arguing, even in disagreements it didn't get out of the way, and most of all he always, always, treated her with the utmost respect. All of this was quite mind blowing to Jayna.

As their relationship grew they learned more and more about one another. Moreover, their agreement about not having sex still remained in tack.

Mark loved Jayna as much as she loved him. He often would come over with dozens of roses, red and white, or just some nice clothes he felt she would look lovely in.

About a year passed by and Jayna still went to praise and worship service. She worshipped the Lord regardless of her outside relationship with Mark. You should know that this is very dangerous because she was treading on Satan's ground. Jayna and Mark bought a home together; of course the two of them having separate bedrooms. Gradually, their relationship grew even stronger but there was one area of Mark's life Jayna was concerned about, his soul. Though he frequented church services his soul had not been saved yet. (He had not willingly given up his will to Jesus to become saved.) This was hard for Jayna because Mark had already started talking about marrying her so they could live together as husband and wife; not as roommates.

One day when Jayna came home from work she noticed the dining room table was set for dinner, for two, with candlelight, roses and orchids. This was not something terribly out of the ordinary because whenever Mark felt extraordinarily loving he would do this. Once he heard Jayna enter into the room he came out of the kitchen to greet her with his normal kiss and hug. Dinner was completely done when she came in. He first sat her down at the well-set table, linen table cloth, china, etcetera, and then he told her to close her eyes to receive the 1st portion of their dinner, to her surprise, he served caviar. Secondly, he served filet mignon, and russet potatoes with sautéed vegetables. To drink he served sparkling cider. Lastly, was the biggest surprise of all for dessert, he told her to close her eyes again, and when she opened them there was a 2carat diamond and sapphire ring on the plate on top of a plain piece of cheese cake. Mark then proceeded to kneel on the floor by her dinner chair and he formally asked her to marry him. Her emotions were mixed because she loved him so much but he had yet to give his whole heart to Jesus but she still said YES! With this thought in mind and the answer she gave him she was still elated by the event but a little sad because she knew if he didn't get saved while they were engaged she would have to call it off.

For the first 2 months of their engagement nothing new seemed to be happening. But in the middle of the third month Mark came to the church's anniversary, where Jayna attended. She was pleased with his decision. Service was really under the anointing power of Jesus that Tuesday nite.

And Mark really seemed to be enjoying himself. All of the sudden it became very obvious how much he was enjoying himself. When the power of God fell upon him and he really let go of what he felt he knew he allowed Jesus to come completely into his heart. This was what Jayna had been praying for all along that he would let go and let Jesus totally in. Jayna was whollistically ecstatic. She knew that at this point she could marry Mark as she had hoped all along.

Nine months later Mark and Jayna were married in a large church nearby their home, with all of their family and friends looking on.

Mark remained very loving toward his new wife for all of about nine months of their marriage.

Eighteen months were now entirely gone and were Mark appeared to have gotten saved thoroughly was now rapidly fading away. How many know this was a trick of deception? To try to lure Jayna away from her walk in Christ, because he knew how much she loved him. (He was being used by Satan and didn't even recognize it).

Beginning with him being rude to Jayna unlike any of the whole relationship they were together. His attendance to church service went from every service to no services at all. He didn't even pray and said so. When she would come home from work she would find him lying around drinking beer and smoking cigarettes. Something he didn't do before. Most of all when they came together as husband and wife, no longer was it loving and pleasurable for Jayna, for the simple reason of Mark always manipulating her. Mentally, physically and emotionally he had a way of making her feel inadequate (saying she was not able to perform her duties as a wife should with her husband) 1 Cor. Chap 7 KJV. Jayna thought to herself, this is a form of rape no matter if he's my husband or not. She also reflected back on how happy she was because Mark had gotten saved. But what she realized most now at this point was that Mark was what she had been praying for but not what Jesus had planned for her life. So it was a matter of dealing with the abuse or just turning her life completely back into Jesus' hands the way it should have been from the beginning. Believing if this was meant to be Jesus would make a way out of no way, seeing to it that Mark would serve Jesus wholly for the rest of his life. Whatever she did she knew she could not divorce him because the Bible clearly states that it's the wrong thing to do. (Matthew 19:3-12, I Corinthians 7:1-14, Matt 5:31-32) KJV.

She fully knew that she was outside of the will of God now. Jayna had allowed her feelings for Mark to camouflage what was really ordained for her life.

<u>Determination</u>

Determination what does it mean? It's having a spirit that doesn't give up, resilience, striving, no one or nothing can stand in your way, its just KNOWING that you can do all things thru Christ who strengthens you.

Attitude in a positive way played a serious part in Kelly's life. Kelly knew that the Lord had great things for her life and they had to be accomplished regardless of what obstacles stood in her way. Many times Satan would try to place men in Kelly's life to hinder her in the path that Christ had laid before her. And the choice was totally up to Kelly because Jesus allows us to make our own decisions.

And there was always a constant battle to get rid of fear of ever being hurt again. To the extent that she knew Jesus would never hurt or harm her in any way but she struggled to give her whole heart to him, that he could move whollistically and miraculously in and thru her, this was her greatest battle. This meant having her will destroyed via Jesus. (Praying with her sincere heart that the spiritual blood clots from all the hurts would be destroyed by the way of his supernatural clot buster, the blood of Jesus, so she would be able to feel his AGAPE love flow through her with his warmth and embrace of love.)

She had to take to heart the word of God that says, "Perfect love (Jesus) casts away all fears" (I John 4:18-19) KJV and to know that with everything in her that Jesus is her best friend and she his.

She came to recognize the draw backs where from previous experiences, which accounted for the hindrances in her ministry: cowardice, sensitivity and caring what people thought, some of this stemmed from the rapes she experienced. Understanding this was a hindrance, she also worked on destroying the very manner of it, by the power of the Holy Spirit, through fasting and praying against it.

Her game plan was to continue to repent, renounce, rebuke and release the Power of God that lived within her, continue in prayer, to keep communication with Jesus and to read the word of God consistently.

In knowing what she had to do, she kept pressing forward to a positive road of recovery (that was no more than allowing Jesus to deliver her completely from any residue of hurts or memories.)
She knew this was a must to have VICTORY thru Jesus Christ.

Resilience played a big part in people laughing at her mishaps. She took them as stepping-stones towards greater accomplishments/Victories. She also realized that all the times she experiences that numbness was a defense that allowed her to keep her right state of mind. It was Jesus.

Though it may seem like Kelly, for a long time, could not see the real deal about men, Jesus allowed these things to be that they would glorify his name thru this story.

Conclusion

One good thing that happened in Kelly's life is that through bible study over the years she learned to trust no man but only to trust Jesus because he will never leave you or forsake you. (Psalms 27, Hebrews 13:5, Psalms 37:25) KJV. Also, that self-esteem is no more than your prideful way that will lead you to fall and will never allow you to give your whole heart to Jesus. In the event you find yourself giving your whole heart to a man it's a form of worship and a big set up from Satan to cause you to fall into the pit of no return. Not being able to go forth in Jesus whole-heartedly, because of it, to tell the whole world how much Jesus loves you and how he's set you free as he did for Kelly.

Kelly and Jayna found out that if you place or allow yourself to be around positive saved people who don't mind encouraging you to do well in the Lord and everyday life you can go very far in your walk for Jesus, knowing that Heaven is your reward.

They both knew that forgiveness had to take place in their deliverance.

They also realized the reality of always learning to give love and then the individual in some manner was no longer in their life. Whether it was family members dying, changing jobs, bonvoyages or just being in a temporary setting, becoming comfortable around those people and then it was time to depart and no longer be around them. Mostly, it was Kelly who could never understand why she always cried when people came in and out of her life. But one day she realized it was because she was still reaching out for love from people.

As she continues on today it is hard not to reach out to people to love them even though they don't always reach back to love her. Her comfort comes when she mediates on the fact that Jesus loves her and not to be concerned about whether people love or care for her.

For Jayna it was a little easier to adjust her emotions.

The devil comes to rape you of your walk in Christ. Even before you find out that Jesus is waiting for you with open arms, to love you. At any time you are violated physically or emotionally that is a form of rape. Rape is an act of seizing and carrying away by force; he (the devil; Satan) can't act or respond intelligently, therefore, he uses one of the oldest acts to destroy you. In the physical, as already mentioned, in many occasions, rape is sex taken by force without consent.

As in all three ladies lives strangers did not do these acts but they were men they knew, associated with or loved.

In the case of, mostly on Jayna's account and some on Kelly's even if you're saved from your sins rape can happen to you if you aren't in the will of the Lord.

It's a matter of just asking Jesus to come into your heart to forgive you of all of your sins, as mentioned with Kelly, then just keeping a real relationship with Jesus that you will know what his will is for your life. By way of prayer and waiting for the answers from him, before go on your way.

Sometimes, depending on the person they may reach out many times for love at a very high price. So you must stay in the will of God.

Hindrances become apart of that price. For certain individuals thinking little of yourself will cause you to continue to allow the same act to happen over and over. And you may even begin to feel others are better than you because you allowed the enemy to lead you in a way that appears to have complete truth, walking out side of the will of God, causing your soundness to become destroyed. It all depends on how much you have allowed yourself to be trapped in this wicked game. You simply have been blinded to what has really been going on. What? A **stronghold** has taken place in your life even as it was for Kelly thus the fasting and praying had to take place. The battle really is on at this point because Satan then believes he had you but you have to keep up the fight in the spirit and he will no longer have a hold on you, no matter how many ways he comes back at you to defeat your purpose in Christ.

Kelly's experience of having said No so many times put her on a road she would not have ever imagined. All she could keep in her mind is <u>No</u> means <u>No</u> from the bottom of her heart, whether he forced himself on her or not, but more often that not. In the United States every minute of the day rape is reported. Over 70% of rapes are known attackers. Two-thirds of women don't report the acts against them.

This conclusion has depicted Kelly and Jayna but Susan was left for last mention simply because she never gave her cares to Jesus that she may become saved, delivered and set free from all of her hurts, disappointments, pains and uncertainties.

There are many Susan's in the world and today I am here to tell you that you can be an <u>**Overcomer**</u> too. Just like Kelly and Jayna. All it takes is for you to give all your burdens to Jesus. But you must do it from the bottom of your heart, all of your mind and soul-which is your personality that makes you who you are today.

Smile Jesus Loves

You

And

So do I.

About the Author

Tonya Jackson is affectionately called Toni by family and friends, a native of Brooklyn, New York raised in Philadelphia, Pennsylvania. She has an identical twin sister, who is 22 minutes older than she is. She attended the Philadelphia public school system for her general education. She then furthered her education in the field of Medical Laboratory Sciences and is currently working as a Lab assistant. She also has completed her Associates Degree in General Studies, received at the Community College of Philadelphia, PA, which will allow her to complete her Bachelor's Degree in the near future.

She came to know the Lord as a young child but didn't receive him wholly until she was an adult. Her spiritual growth and development for her Christian walk is received at the New Faith Non- Denominational House of Prayer in Philadelphia, Pennsylvania.

Her goal is to reach the masses of people who will allow themselves to acknowledge that they need comfort, love and peace in the spirit, through Christ Jesus.

LaVergne, TN USA
15 August 2010
193344LV00002B/133/A